Emily's Tiger

Dedicated to Hannah, love from Mimi xx — M. L.

Barefoot Books
2067 Massachusetts Ave
Cambridge, MA 02140

Text and illustrations copyright © 2008 by Miriam Latimer
The moral right of Miriam Latimer to be identified as the author and illustrator of this work has been asserted

First published in the United States of America in 2008 by Barefoot Books, Inc.
This paperback edition first published in 2011

This book has been printed on 100% acid-free paper

Graphic design by Judy Linard, London
Color separation by Grafiscan, Verona
Printed and bound in China by Printplus Ltd

This book was typeset in Zemke Hand ITC 24 and 65 on 33 point
The illustrations were prepared in acrylics and collage

Library of Congress Cataloging-in-Publication Data:

Emily's tiger / [text and illustrations by] Miriam Latimer.

p. cm.

Summary: Emily always lets her inner tiger roar when things do not go
her way until her grandmother shows her how to turn her angry tiger into
a happy one.

ISBN 978-1-84686-594-7 (hardcover : alk. paper)

[1. Temper tantrums--Fiction. 2. Behavior--Fiction. 3.
Grandmothers--Fiction.] I. Title.
PZ7.L369625Em 2008 [E]--dc22 2007025040

57986

Emily's Tiger

Miriam Latimer

Barefoot Books
Celebrating Art and Story

"I don't want my hair cut,"
Emily pouted.

"Emily, please sit down,"
Mom sighed.

"NO!"

Emily growled
and then . . .

. . . she gave her loudest tiger ROAR!
"Not again!" Mom groaned.
"Come here, you rascal!"
Emily bounded around the room,
and bounced out of the window.

"Oh, Emily," Mom sighed again.
"What are we going to do with you?"

Later, at Evie's party, the clown announced, "I need an assistant."

"Me!" squealed Emily.

"I choose Evie, the birthday girl,"
said the clown.

"But I want to be the helper!"
growled Emily.

The clown shook his head.
Emily stamped her foot and gave
a huge . . .

ROAR!

Soon Evie's party was in chaos.

"Oh, Emily," sighed Dad when he came to take her home. "What are we going to do with you?"

At dinnertime, Dad tried to persuade
Emily to eat some carrots.

"I don't like carrots!" Emily snapped, and swishing her long, curly tail, she swiped her plate right up into the air.

"Oh, Emily!" groaned Mom. Just then, the doorbell rang.

"Hello, I'm here!" sang Granny as she pranced through the door. "Gollygumdrops, it looks like a zoo in here. What's been going on?"

"I got upset, Granny. I don't like carrots." Emily hung her head.

"Oh, Emily," smiled Granny, "What are we going to do with you? I know, let's go upstairs."

"I want to share a secret with you," whispered Granny. She turned away and when she looked back, Granny gave a loud tiger . . .

ROAR!

"Eeek!" Emily jumped back in surprise.

"No need to be scared, pumpkin," Granny assured her. "I only turn into a tiger when I want to. That way, I can turn myself into a happy tiger instead of an angry one. And happy tigers have much more fun."

That night, Emily dreamt about being a tiger with Granny.

Together, they leapt all the way along the roofs of the cars that were parked on Emily's street.

"Higher?" asked Granny. Emily nodded, and they leapt all the way along the roofs of the houses.

"Higher?" asked Granny. Emily nodded, and Granny leapt right over the moon. Emily didn't dare follow her there.

"How did you do that?" she asked.

"You'll learn." Granny smiled.

"Have you brushed your teeth yet?"
Mom asked Emily in the morning.
"I hate brushing my teeth!"
said Emily.
"I love brushing mine,"
whispered Granny.

Emily decided to brush
her teeth to shine just
like Granny's.

After school, Granny and Emily went to the park. Emily spotted Dylan Jones making a fort.

"Can I help?" asked Emily.

But as she peeped inside Dylan's tent, he climbed onto her bike and began riding it around the park.

"Hey, give it back!" shouted Emily, and she crouched down, ready to pounce.

Then she glimpsed over at
Granny. Her big paws were
wrapped around
a book. She
looked very
relaxed.

Emily decided to relax, just like Granny.
"Yippee!" Dylan whooped as he pedaled
past. Emily ignored him.

Dylan tried riding with no hands. He lost
his balance and fell off.

"Wahhh!" he yelled.

Emily helped Dylan pick himself up.
"Are you OK?"
she asked.

Granny grinned
and gave Emily
a big thumbs-up.

At dinnertime, Emily ate all of her carrots — just like Granny.

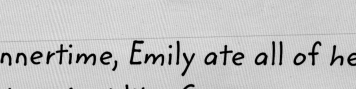

She helped Dad wash up, and she brushed
her teeth without even the slightest growl.

Later on, there was a rat-tat-tat-tat on Emily's bedroom door.

"Psst!" whispered Granny. "Follow me." And they crept outside.

"Now for the fun part," said Granny.
"Come on, Emily!" she called as she
fearlessly hurdled the backyard fence.
She showed Emily how to soar
over hedges, scale walls
and climb trees.

"Happy tiger or angry tiger?"
asked Granny.

"Happy tiger!" cried Emily,
and then she jumped right
over the moon.